SADDLED

TAIWO EUNICE BEJIDE

DEDICATION

This Book is Dedicated to my Lovely Dad and Mum, Mr&Mrs Bejide Victor..

CONTENTS

CHARACTERS

FEMI------- MR ADEJOBI'S SON
MR ADEJOBI---- A WEALTHY ILLITERATE
MR OLA------- A CAR DEALER
MRS OLA----- MR OLA'S WIFE
KUNLE------ MR OLA'S SON
TINU-------- MR OLA'S DAUGHTER
MR JERRY------ MR ADEJOBI'S FRIEND
MR JUMO----- SS3 MATHEMATICS TEACHER
KEJI-------- MR ADEJOBI'S DRIVER
KOLA------- MR ADEJOBI'S GATEKEEPER
TISI--------- MR ADEJOBI'S COOK
MR SMITH------ THE SS1 ENGLISH TEACHER
FASH------- KUNLE'S CLASSMATE
ABBEY------- FEMI'S CLASSMATE
MR SAM------- SS1 LITERATURE TEACHER
MR OYE-------ST. JUDE SEC. SCHOOL
PRINCIPAL
MR BENSON----ONE OF MR ADEJOBI'S
WORKERS

ACT 1 SCENE 1

[In Mr. Adejobi's Residence,a large compound painted in white with lots of rooms in it, the sitting room has a small glass table surrounded by beautiful chairs, Mr Adejobi's favourite sound-set is seen at one corner of the room arranged on a shelf at the front side of the sitting-room the sound of music from the sound set fills the air]
Mr Adejobi: A bright day indeed! I wish everyday could be as interesting, I am sure my son will be proud of me.
[A knock bangs at door] Yes, come in,
[Mr Jerry enters]

Mr jerry: Hi kole, you put up a fantastic show at your son's birthday party, I never knew you could do that for him..

Mr Adejobi: *[slightly upset]* what do you mean? Are you insinuating I could never have done that or what?

Mr Jerry: I hope you understand me Kole, you're are wealthy, yet you refused your son the right to formal education, don't you think this is wickedness? The poor boy cries day and night craving that knowledge obtained through formal education yet you refused him and you're here thinking that by organizing him a birthday party he will be very proud of you? You think you are a proud father?

Mr Adejobi: Jerry are you here to insult me? I thought you should be here sharing me some accolades, but if you've come all the way here to insult me then get out of my house!

Mr Jerry: *[with a calm voice]* I don't mean any offence Kole, and I'm sorry if my words sounds harsh but I hope you would see the truth in what I'm telling you and…I have always wanted to ask you this question..

Mr Adejobi: Ok go on, if it's a reasonable one.

Mr Jerry : I won't mind that, but this is my question., Why did you refuse to educate your son? He is your only son, as well as your only child and you're one of the famous and richest men in this state, but why did you choose to do this to your son?

Mr Adejobi: Now you are talking! You should have asked the question first, you see, children with formal education these days are proud and they have no regard for anyone not even their own parents, I will not allow my son to be like that. Never!

Mr Jerry: What do you mean?

Mr Adejobi: Don't you see Mr Jaye's son? The boy was educated to a satisfactory level by his parents but what did he turn out to be? He now despises his parents, he has a well-paid job now, in fact he is even the MD [Managing Director] to a big company, but he will never check on his parents, didn't know how they were faring, he only calls once in a blue moon, and anytime they wanted him to come home, he gives lame excuses and tells them he here is busy and won't be able to come, he travels within and outside the country at will, but will never come over to see his parents, all I do is pity his pathetic parent who remains poor and had to cater for themselves with no hope of surviving even when they had a well-to-do son somewhere, Now, you're telling me to make the same mistake Mr Jaye made?, To send my son to school, so he could forget me? Never! It's better he learns the trade I want him to learn and make money with that, Children with formal education this days are often arrogant. Just take a good look at me, I was only educated to basics six[6] after which I stopped schooling because I realized it is of no use, My parents were one of the wealthiest in the country, and I inherited their properties and I am rich so Femi too will inherit my properties when I'm old and gone.

Mr Jerry: You made your point Kole, but you can't look at the negative side of things alone without looking at the positive, what about the children that were educated and took good care of their parents and families? why is it that you only saw Mr Jaye's part!

Mr Adejobi: Well, I have not seen children like that, all I know is that, even when parents train them and give them formal education, they end of focusing on the family they build later, their wife and children, and forget the family that made them what they are, and this is mostly common to the male children, that is what formal education teaches them to do, and I will never allow my son do the same to me.

Mr Jerry: I have told you to look at the positive side of things, Kole! please take away all these ideas in your head and reason positively, Femi is now 17 and he's still learning trade, for God's sake educate this boy, He has the passion to study!

Mr Adejobi: *[Sighs]* I've heard you then, you just want me to send Femi to school, ok I'll think about it.

Mr Jerry: Think wisely please, I want to take my leave now. *[moves towards the door]*

Mr Adejobi: [Refuse to escort his friend, sits still on the sofa] ok bye!

ACT 1 SCENE 2

[Femi is in his room, cleaning and putting some things in order; Mr Adejobi enters, clears his throat to get Femi's attention but Femi ignores his presence]

Mr Adejobi: Oh Femi, you are here?

Femi: Yes Dad,

Mr Adejobi: Your party today is one of its kind, it will be the talk of the town, you should thank me for that.

Femi: Good afternoon dad.

Mr Adejobi: *[slightly upset]* Is that what you will say? You heard everything I said, don't try to ignore it.

Femi: But why Dad, why are you disturbing me? Just let me be please!

Mr Adejobi: *[surprised]* Femi!

Femi: I should thank you for the birthday party right? I told you I don't want this party in the first place, but you insisted, you wanted it, to show yourself I suppose; with all those money you sprayed and squandered, You were spraying money all around, why can't you use all those money for my education? All I wanted is to have a formal education, not a birthday party! *[burst into tears]* but No, you didn't do that, you preferred to lavish the money on a birthday party; I want to ask you a question Dad..

Mr Adejobi: what is it my son?

Femi: Did I just hear you say my son? Hope that wasn't a mistake, Mr Kole?

Mr Adejobi:*[surprised]* So, Femi! you're now so angry that you called my name instead of Dad? I will not be disrespected by my own son, and hope you haven't forgotten the scriptures that told you to honour your father and mother so that your days will be long..

Femi: Oh Dad! So now you quote the scriptures, you knew the scriptures but you choose to be wicked even to your own son? So have you also forgotten so fast that the scriptures all tells fathers not to provoke their son so that they won't be discouraged? And for your information dad, I didn't disrespect you anyway

Mr Adejobi: *[Angry]* it is as though you've been moving with some gangs right? what did you expect me to do? I made you learn a trade and you said I am wicked right? So have you forgotten that what an elder sees sitting, a child cannot see even if he climbs the longest tree?

[Femi didn't respond, he was busy with his arrangement] You won't respond right? You want to prove stubborn, No matter what you do, I won't have you go to school, I won't let you turn me into a laughing stock to the society, never!

Femi: *[Taken aback by his father's statement; wipes his tears]* So be it! If you harden your heart and won't have me educated so be it! Suit yourself! *[He kept arranging his things and refused to say a word until his father left the room in annoyance; (soliloquizing)]* what kind of life is this? I am 17, some of my mates are writing their O'levels, yet my own father refused me education despite how wealthy he is, I'll keep pushing I owe myself what I become, and I know what to do.

Mr Adejobi: *[in the sitting room, talking to himself]* imagine! So my own son is now upset with me? No way! No matter what he does, I won't educate him, he will be like that and learn good morals not the arrogance of the literates *[He suddenly saw Femi with a bag containing his baggage moving down the stairs; he's surprised]* Femi where do you think you're going ? *[He didn't respond, instead, he kept moving down the stairs towards the door]* Femi are you deaf? I said come back here! Did you also want to leave me like your mother did?

Femi: *[looks back at his father]* what? You said my mother left you? You can say that again, you turned her into your punching bag, maltreated her; No she won't leave, she will stay with you and continue suffering till you kill her.

Mr Adejobi: Say whatever you want, but you are not leaving this house today,
[Mr Adejobi rushes towards Femi, collects his bags forcefully and locked him up in a room] You think you can leave like that! No, stay in that room and think about it, you are not going anywhere, disobedient brat!

Curtain

falls

ACT 2

[Mr Ola, A car dealer is seen sitting in the sitting room with his wife and childeren listening to the news at night]

Mr ola: I don't know what the country is becoming, there are lots of natural resources but the administration seems to be damning.

Mrs Ola: Its upsetting dear, but I pray the Almighty intervenes

Tinu: what dad said is right

Mr Ola: *[Turns to his wife]* what about dinner dear, I'm starving

Mrs Ola: Dinner will soon be ready dear please be patient

Kunle: Mum please be fast about the food, I'm hungry

Mrs Ola: *[gave him a scornful look]* If you had been of help in the kitchen just like your sister, dinner would be ready by now! Stand up now and fetch me two buckets of water!

Kunle: *[stands up reluctantly and moves out to fetch the water]* Ok ma

Mr ola : You should have come home earlier dear, stop being harsh on my son

Mrs Ola: He is also my son and I'm sorry for the late dinner.

Mr Ola: No problem dear, but please…… [robs his stomach]

Mrs Ola: *[Smiles}* I understand, just a little bit more please *[goes into the kitchen]*

ACT 2 SCENE 2

[Femi, walking on the street is lost in deep thought and didn't notice a vehicle coming behind him, horning at him, the driver alighted from the vehicle and walked towards him and stood behind him for some minute, but he was so lost in thought that he didn't notice all this]

Mr Ola: *[finally speaks]* Hello young man, *[didn't get a response; taps him]* Young Man!

Femi: *[recovers]* Oh…..Good morning sir,

Mr Ola: What's the matter with you? I have been horning for quite some time and I've been at your back watching you for some couple minutes now, but you seemed not to notice all these, what's the matter with you?

Femi: oh..really I'm sorry sir
[attempts to leave]

Mr Ola: *[Holds him back]* what is wrong with you boy, why are you so lost in thought?

Femi: Nothing sir, I'm sorry

Mr Ola: Boy, you don't need to be shy and don't see me as a bad person you can talk to me, what is the matter with you?

Femi: I'm sorry for being carried away on the street like this, I'm sincerely sorry *[still intends to leave]*

Mr Ola: *[Holds him back]* Is something bothering you young man? Please talk to me as you know a problem shared is half solved, I might be of help to you and at least I am old enough to be your father.

Femi: I'm sorry if I've being rude sir, it wasn't intentional.

Mr Ola: oh boy come on, I wasn't saying you were rude, I was just saying that you can talk to me, I want to know why a young boy like you is here at this hour of the day, carried away in his thoughts when he is supposed to be in school.

Femi: *[Bursts into uncontrollable tears and tries to wipe them as it falls]* ok, I will tell you, but then, you were on your way going somewhere before you met me and I wouldn't want to delay you, so we can talk some other time, just .....

Mr Ola: *[Interrupts]* Of course I was on my way to the office, but then that can wait, I am a car dealer and I own the business, I have some assistant, they will be there by now, so you can see, you are not delaying me in any way, so let's find a place to sit and talk about everything, why you are here at this time, and that burden in your heart.. *[they both sat under a shade nearby to discuss]*

Femi: Sir my name is Femi Adejobi

Mr Ola: Adejobi Adejobi... That name sounds familiar, Which Adejobi please?

Femi: Bankole Adejobi's son

Mr Ola: *[Shocked]* Bankole Adejobi, the one living in Adejobi street? Owner of Baki filling station, Baki oil and gas? only to mention a few?

Femi: Yes sir

Mr Ola: Oh, how are you? You shouldn't be here at this time, your father is famous and rich, you should...

Femi: *[interrupts]* Of course, my father is famous and rich but he doesn't know the value of education, he's ignorant!

Mr Ola: *[surprised!]* …for him to be as rich,.. he must have been educated and intelligent!
Femi: Oh! You think so? well, he just inherited all the wealth from his parents, his father who happened to be my grandfather was one of the wealthiest in the state, and my father was the only son of the man, he was compelled to have a formal education but he always insists that education wasn't meant for him as he didn't take education serious and at some point he stopped schooling and refused to listen to the plea of his parents, So you see, he is extending that ignorance towards me, as he refused to have me go to school, claiming that I will inherit his property after he is old and gone, I'm just tired of this!

Mr Ola: Really!..but you sound educated, in words, the way you speak, your…

Femi: *[interrupts]* My father had me learn a trade, photography precisely, he assigned me as an apprentice to one of his friends who is a photographer, so because of his ignorance he thought that was what I've been learning all the while.

Mr Ola: what to do you mean?

Femi: *[continues]* He bought me a very expensive camera at age five (5), he didn't even notice that I couldn't use it at that age, but thank God for his friend, Mr Jerry, he has really been a help to me, he helped me with that camera and enrolled me in a nursery school, I started schooling at age 5 and he has been helping me make good use of the camera, I left the camera in his care because he's a photographer, my father had wanted me to learn from him, so he's my boss, but the upgraded version of camera my father bought me which a middle-class man couldn't afford, it gave a boost to his profession as a photographer and he's been more money with it, but then he gives me 40 percent of everything he makes, knowing fully well that I have no passion for photography but education, he enrolled me in a school and cater for all my needs, all this he did without the knowledge of my father, He Is God's sent to me

Mr Ola: hmm..that is so thoughtful of him, he is a good man, and he's your Dad's friend?

Femi: Yes sir, you would have heard about him, he published magazines on tourism, documentaries encyclopedia... he is a great photographer, but I don't have passion for that photography, not without education. what gives me the hardest moment of life now is that Mr Jerry has been sick for some weeks now and I just went to check on him, that's where I was coming from when we met, I pray he gets well soon, honestly things has been very tough without him especially in aspect of my education.

Mr Ola: You are wonderful boy, I am so sorry you have to go through all this, you are passionate about education and you are ambitious, I will love to help you in the little way that I can, I am also blessed with two children a boy and a girl, my boy is preparing for his senior secondary school three, almost about to write the senior secondary exam, and my daughter Tinu is in the senior secondary school one, just like you, please take *[hands Femi a complementary card]* you can come to me, my address is there and my phone number, please look for me I'll be glad to help you in the little way I can.

Femi: Thank you very much sir, I really appreciate you, thanks for your time and the listening ear you granted me, Thank you, God bless you!

Mr Ola: [enters into his car, and zoomed off] okay bye

ACT   2   SCENE   3

[In Mr Adejobi's house, Femi got home around 3:30 p.m. in the afternoon]

Mr Adejobi: Femi you came home early today, hope there is no issue?

Femi: No Dad *[Walking into his room]*

Mr Adejobi: Femi, come back here, I demand an explanation don't you think?
Femi: what explanation?

Mr Adejobi: The reason you came home early

Femi: I'm just tired, that that's all

Mr Adejobi: So that's it, that's an excuse right? Well that excuse is lame I won't accept it *[Femi stood there, looked at his father in amusement and just walked into his room]*

Mr Adejobi: Okay we shall see

Femi: *[In his room]* Oh, God! What kind of life is this? I got home 3:30 p.m. instead of 4 p.m. and this man*(his dad)* complains that I got home early,?

Curtain

falls

ACT 3

SCENE 1

[After dinner in Mr Ola's house, he sits in the living room with his wife and children]

Mr Ola: Honey guess what?

Mrs Ola: What is it dear?

Mr Ola: Can you imagine?

Mrs Ola: What is it dear?

Mr Ola: On my way to the office today, I saw a young man, who was so deep in thought that he didn't notice that my car was coming behind, thank goodness I was very careful with my driving.

Mrs Ola: Thank God, but dear, what could have been the matter with him?

Mr Ola: I alighted from my car and moved closer to him, I watched him from behind then tapped his shoulder and that was when he recovered in fear.

Kunle: Is the boy deaf?

Mr Ola: Oh, he is not!

Tinu: Why are you telling us this Dad?

Mrs Ola: Will you just shut up and listen to your father!

Tinu: I am sorry dad
Mr Ola: The boy was Femi Adejobi the wealthy Mr Adejobi's son
Kunle: Wow, why was he lost in thought what was he thinking about?

Tinu: Your questions are just too much just let Dad talk!

Mr Ola: *[Faces his children in annoyance]* I shouldn't have brought you both into this discussion in the first place but I thought you might also bring ideas on how to go about things, but now you're making everything complicated than I expected.

Kunle & Tinu: We are sorry Dad.

Mr Ola: Just keep quiet and listen! Alright as I was saying dear, could you believe that this man does not know the value of education and as a result of this refused to send his son to school?

Mrs Ola: Really!

Mr Ola: Yes, instead he bought the boy a high quality and expensive camera and signed him into a trade to become a photographer?

Kunle: Oh no! how can...[his father gave him a scornful look] I'm sorry sir

Mrs Ola: He is educated himself, so he should know the value of one
Mr Ola: why do you think so?

Mrs Ola: come on darling, everyone knows he is one of the richest in this state as well as the country, he owns big companies and filling stations, industries....

Mr Ola: [interrupts with laughter] I also had the same thought, but why communing with his son today, I discovered that he stopped schooling at basic (6) six

Mrs Ola: *[shocked]* You don't mean it! how come? so how did he amass all those wealth?

Mr Ola: According to the boy, he inherited it from his rich parents, their grandparents were very rich and they own all the companies, and the father was their only son, he was unserious with education because he thought his parents wealth was enough, he dropped out of school at basic six, at such a lower-level, claiming that education isn't for him although the grandparents which happens to be the father's parents persuaded their son to be serious with his education but all to no avail.

Kunle: Hmm...

Mr Ola: So the man also thought, that just as he had inherited the wealth from his parents, his son will also inherit his wealth

Mrs Ola: This is ridiculous!

Mr Ola: *[nods]*....but as for the boy, I have never met someone so wise, He is very passionate about his education and also brilliant, although his father didn't send him to school but he sent himself he educated himself!

Tinu: How Dad?

Mr Ola: With the help of his father's friend, although according to him, the man isn't as rich as his father but being a close friend to his father, when he learnt that the man bought a camera for his son to make him a photographer instead of sending him to school, he decided to help him.

Mrs Ola: How did he do that dear?

Mr Ola: The father's friend was a photographer by profession, so the father thought it wise for his son to be trained by his friend, but the friend collected the camera from the boy and works with it, he publish magazines on tourism, documentaries, encyclopedias etc.

and makes money with it, when the boy resume work by 7:30 every morning, he prepares him to go to school, but on weekends like Saturdays he teaches the boy about photography!

Mrs Ola: Oh that's great, friends like that are one in a million!

Mr Ola: You can say that again dear, but the man, I mean his father's friend has been sick for a few weeks now which was the reason for the boy's emotional down-cast, but I also assured him that I will help him in the little way that I can

Mrs Ola: That's good dear, God bless you!

Mr Ola: *[smiles at his wife]* Thanks for being a kind, understanding and sweet woman!

[They   all   laughed]

ACT 3 SCENE 2

[In Mr Adejobi's compound, Femi and Keji the driver is having a conversation]

Femi: Thanks alot Keji

Keji: Why? why the appreciation all of a sudden?

Femi: You don't understand what you keep doing for me, you've been the only one who knows about me, yet you didn't tell my dad about this, you kept driving me to school when you were instructed to drive me to work and from there, you always wait till I got prepared for school and you drive me to school, I really appreciate you, thank you very much.

Keji: That's enough Femi! It's my pleasure, I am really glad that at least, I could do that for you, God will continue to help you..

Femi: Amen, thank you

Keji: I could remember that just like you I was very passionate about formal education, although I had a very humble background but my parents at least had me go to school, but when they were no longer capable of paying the tuition I dropped out but I'm glad today that I could help you.

Femi: it's okay Keji, I understand *[Femi remembers quickly that he needed to visit Mr Ola who has given him his address then he rushed in to change his clothes preparing to go to Mr ola's house, his father who was in the sitting room seeing him rush in and out of his room questioned him]*

Mr Adejobi: where are you heading?

Femi: A friend's house

Mr Adejobi: And you don't think you should inform me before going?

Femi: I'm sorry sir, now you know [making to leave]

Mr Adejobi: I want you to spend some time with me

Femi: Doing what?

Mr Adejobi: Spend some time with your father, let's have fun, come, let's play the Ludo game together

Femi: I'm sorry Dad, I can't, I'm in a hurry

Mr Adejobi: *[shouts!]* …And where are you going that is more important than your father?

Femi: *[Turns to look at his father]* Indeed! *[turns back to the door, open it and leaves the room, got to the compound gate but it was locked, he calls to gatekeeper]* Kola! Kola!

Kola: Yes sir

Femi: open the gate!

Kola: No, please, I can't

Femi: *[surprised!]* what?! Why?!

Kola: Your Dad said I shouldn't let you out of the compound.

Femi: *[Annoyed]* My father said that? Open the gate now!

Kola: [*Fidgeting*] please Femi, don't let me open the gate, I'll get fired if I do!
[Mr Adejobi comes out from the room and watches them from behind, but Femi ignores him]

Femi: I said, open this gate!.. before I count to three... one...

Kola: *[prostrates and holds his leg]* Femi please!

Femi: *[looks at his father where he was standing and turns back to kola]* what if I get you fired instead? because if my father doesn't, I definitely will

Kola: [*still prostrating*] please Femi don't make me open the gate, help me please
[Femi walks into the gatekeeper's apartment, which was closer to the gate, picked the key to the gate and was about opening the gate]
Mr Adejobi: *[shouts]* Kola, you must not let him out or you're fired!

Kola: *[kneels with tears rolling down his cheeks]* please Femi, don't do this please, I have families to feed!

Femi: *[moved with sympathy towards kola, he closed back the gate and handed him the key; faces his father]* I did this for him [He went back into the house, into his room.

Curtain falls

ACT 4

SCENE 1

[Femi picks Mr Ola's address to go visit one Saturday]

Femi: *[knocks]* Hello!

Kunle: *[opens the door]* Hello!

Femi: Good afternoon, My name is Femi and I'm here to see Mister Ola

Kunle: ok, come in

Femi: Thanks

Kunle: Welcome

Femi: *[Greets Mr and Mrs Ola who were both in the sitting room]* Good afternoon sir and ma

Mrs Ola: Good afternoon dear

Mr Ola: Oh Femi, how are you? Now you've decided to come visit me, that's good, I've always expected you, how's everything?

Femi: I'm fine sir, everything is well

Mr Ola: Your Dad? Femi: He's fine too.

Mr Ola: [Turns to his wife] This is Femi, the boy I told you about,.Mr Adejobi's son..

Mrs Ola: oh .. Femi, you're welcome, how are you dear, how's your Dad and Mom?
Femi: we're fine, thanks ma

Mrs Ola: It's good to have you around

Femi: It's nice to meet you too ma..
[Mrs Ola goes into the kitchen to prepare lunch for the family and the visitor]

Mr Ola: so how're you Femi?

Femi: I'm good sir

Mr Ola: *[phone rings]* Excuse me please, *[Mr Ola excused himself to receive the confidential call, Kunle and Femi was left alone in the sitting room; then after few minutes of silence, kunle decided to start a conversation]*

Kunle: Your Dad is rich right?

Femi: *[ignores the question and diverts the discussion to kunle's picture on the wall]* That picture is nice, you're really wonderful in native attire.

Kunle: oh you recognize me?

Femi: *[surprised]* what do you mean?

Kunle: I just find it hard to believe that you could recognize me in that picture, the picture was taken when I was younger, and most people that come to our house for the first time like this, often find it difficult to recognize me in it.

Femi: *[calmly]* is that so?

Kunle: Yes

Femi: Ok *[There was some minute of silence once again in the room before kunle interrupts the the silence]*

Kunle: But why don't you smile Femi?
Femi: *[confused]* what? kunle: I just noticed that ever since we've been on this discussion you didn't smile

Femi: *[surprised]* Oh really I'm sorry, probably the situation doesn't call for it.

Kunle: No not that, even when I tried to crack some jokes yet you...

Tinu: *[Comes out from the kitchen]* Kunle food is ready.

Kunle: okay *[Lunch was served and the family ate happily together]*
[After lunch]

Mr Ola: Femi, I want to have some words with you, Kunle and Tinu please excuse us. *[kunle and Tinu left the dining room to their various rooms leaving Mr ola, their Mum and Femi behind]* How're going about schooling now?

Femi: I'm trying my best sir

Mr Ola: And your father's friend, how is he?

Femi: He's recovering

Mr Ola: Thank God, and don't forget that I told you, that if you ever need my assistance, don't hesitate to let me know

Femi: Thank you sir

Mrs Ola: Oh dear, I heard all that happened to you, I'm sorry you have to go through this, but keep being strong, and don't give up, then success is yours, God will continue to help you

Femi: Amen, thank you ma, thanks for the motherly advice, thank you sir, thank you both [prostrates for the first time]

Mr & Mrs ola: Don't mention dear.

ACT 4 SCENE 2

[Femi arrived at 6 p.m. from Mr Ola's house and his father Mr Adejobi becomes worried about this]

Mr Adejobi: *[In this room; Soliloquizing]* Where could Femi go, by this hour of the night this is 6 p.m. and he's not yet home, *[He kept on pacing, then he called on all his workers and told them to be on the lookout, then he went into his room and laid on his bed restless] [A knock bangs at the gate and Kola rushes to open it; Femi enters]*

Kola: Welcome, why are you just coming by this time, your father has been worried

Femi: Really! Worried about what?

Kola: Worried about you of course, that you weren't home yet
Femi: is that so?

Kola: Why all these questions? I thought you will just rush in to meet your...

Femi: *[interrupts]* Will you shut up!

Kola: I'm sorry Femi: Who do you think you are to tell me what to do? What will transpire between me and my dad, if I'll rush to meet him or not is none of your business!, Do you understand?

Kola: Yes sir, I'm sorry
[Mr Adejobi comes out of his room after hearing his distant conversations and seeing them through the CCTV camera in his room]

Mr Adejobi: Femi, what's the problem and why are you just returning home by this time?

Femi: Good evening Dad

Mr Adejobi: Evening! This is night! and don't even dare to ignore my question with the greeting; I said why are you coming home this late today?

Femi: *[upset]* Just leave me alone Dad! this is just 6 p.m. for God's sake! the day I returned home by 3:30 p.m. you said it was too early and now, a little bit past 6 p.m. is too late?

Kola: *[Tries to hold Femi's hand to tell him to be gentle]* Femi your Dad...

Femi: *[Turns to kola]*...And.. Let me knock a good deal of nonsense off your head today , The next time I am having a conversation with my Dad, try and much as possible to keep your mouth shut, Cos it's none of your business!

Kola: I'm sorry, I'm just trying to...

Femi: *[interrupts]* Get out of my sight!
[kola leaves and Femi storms into the house in annoyance, Mr Adejobi follows]

Curtain fall

ACT 5

SCENE 1

[Femi had a change of school with the help of Mr and Mrs ola, he now attends sent Jude secondary school, the same school with kunle and Tinu, kunle is in senior secondary 3 while Femi and Tinu are both in senior secondary 1; Mr Smith the English teacher enters the SS1 class, and the students salute]

Mr Smith: Happy resumption to you all

Class: thank you sir

Mr Smith: I know you are enjoying the holiday, so with this I will test you to know if you haven't eaten away all I have thought you, can anyone tell me what he/she knows about the vowel sound? *[Hands were raised and the teacher looks around to call on anyone]* You!

Femi: Me?

Mr Smith: Yes this is the first time I will see you in this class, may I know you?

Femi: My name is Femi Adejobi and I am a new student

Mr Smith: Ok I see, well answer the question

Femi: Sir

Mr Smith: You heard me, I said answer the question, I know you are a new student but I want to know your ability, what is the vowel sound?

Femi: Vowel sounds are sounds produced when there is no obstruction to the air coming from the vocal tract

Mr Smith: *[amazed]* Yes correct, but apart from the definition what else can you tell us about the vowel sound?

Femi: Vowel sound in English language are 20 in number and this 20 sounds can be divided into two categories which are the 12 pure vowels sounds also known as the Monophthongs and the 8 diphthongs which are also called gliding vowels.

Mr Smith: A round of applause for him please, *[The class applauds him]* you can have your seat that's really good of you

Femi: *[Bows and sits]* Thank you sir

Mr Smith: So, now, who can tell me about the consonant sound apart from the definition [No hand was raised]Abbey can you try ?

Abbey: *[With a shaky voice]* c-o-n-s-o-nant so--ou--nd is a word…

Mr Smith: *[Dissapointed]* So you don't know what the consonant sound is? Afterall, I thought you last term! Who else can try?.........No one? This is ridiculous! Ok new student, can you try, please?

Femi: *[Stands]* Consonant sounds are sounds produced when there's obstruction to the air coming from the vocal cord; consonant sounds in English language are twenty-four{24} in number and can also be divided into the voiced and voiceless; it could also be classified with thee important factors which are; THE Place of Articulation, Manner of Articulation and the State or Position of the glottis.. The place of articulation are the specific place where the production of sound takes place, the manner of articulation shows how…. *[The class interrupts with applauds]*

Mr Smith: Wow! This is good! Which school did you transfer from?

Femi: Ultimate Sec. School, sir

Mr Smith: ..And your name again?

Femi: Femi Adejobi

Mr Smith: I must confess, you're really wonderful Femi, please have your sit!

Femi: *[sits]* Thanks sir,

Mr Smith: Ok Class let's call it a day!

ACT   5   SCENE   2

[It is closing hour and all the students were leaving the school for their various houses, kunle came to call Tinu in class]

Kunle: Tinu, Why are you still sitting here, let's go home dad might be waiting

Tinu: We both know dad can't be here yet,

Kunle: Then let's go wait for him *[sights Femi]* Femi what's up?! Are you not going home too?

Femi: Oh, not yet, thanks

Kunle: why?

Femi: Nothing

Kunle: *[smiles]* And by the way, Femi how's your first day, in the school, hope you like it here?

Femi: Absolutely

Kunle: it's nice to hear that, ok then, let's go home now, dad will come pick us up soon

Femi: Thanks for the kind gesture, but I'm sorry I can't just go home yet

Kunle & Tinu *[surprised]* Why?!

Femi: *[Amazed]* I thought you should understand, this is 2pm, I can't go home until 4pm at least to convince my dad who still thinks I am an apprentice whose closing hour is 4:00pm, until that time, I can't go home, in order to avoid his dramas.

Kunle: Oh, I now understand!

Femi: Good, so extend my greetings to your parent

Kunle &Tinu: Ok bye, *[they both leave the classroom]*

ACT   5   SCENE   3

[Mr ola arrived at the school to pick his children]

Tinu& Kunle: Welcome Dad

Mr Ola: Welcome children, how's school today?

Tinu & kunle: School's fine Dad

Mr Ola: Good! Ok let's go… Oh where's Femi?

Tinu: He's still in the classroom

Mr Ola: Doing what? Why didn't he come along with you so I could drop him at home..?

Tinu: He said he can't go home yet, to avoid his father's drama and to prevent him from knowing what's up

Mr Ola: ok, go call him *[kunle goes into Femi's class room to call him; on arrival;]*

Femi: Good afternoon sir

Mr Ola: Good afternoon dear, how're you?

Femi: I'm good sir, and you?

Mr Ola: Oh, Very well, I'm fine, and how's your first day here at saint Jude? Femi: it's fine sir

Mr Ola: *[with a little frown]*Ehn--femi, I heard you don't want to go home yet, for some reasons, but then, why don't you come stay with us till 4pm, then you can go home, or possibly, I can drop you at home by then myself, how about that?

Femi: Thank you sir, but I've made an arrangement with my driver to come pick me here by 4pm

Mr Ola: Your driver?

Femi: Yes, he is aware of everything, he usually come pick me at my former school too;

Mr Ola: So that shows that your driver knows so much about you.

Femi:*[nods]*Yes sir

Mr Ola: Very well then, you can send him my home address right now, he will come pick you up there, you can't stay in school alone till 4:pm

Femi: Ok sir, I'll do that, thanks alot sir *[They all got into the car and Mr Ola drove them home]*

ACT 5 SCENE 4

[At Mr Ola's residence]

Tinu &Kunle: Good afternoon Mum

Mrs Ola: Welcome my children, Femi how're you?

Femi: I am good, Good afternoon ma

Mrs Ola: How's school today, my children?

Tinu & Kunle: Children!? We are no longer children, mum we are grown- ups now

Mrs Ola: *[smiles]* How are you today grown-ups? [They all laughed], Go freshen up, eat and relax for some minutes we have some chores to do.

Kunle: No mum, let's do the chores first so we can then sit down to eat our food in peace

Tinu: I agree mum!

Mrs Ola: Oh ok then, if that is what you want, you don't have much chores anyways, you just need to fetch some waters into the jars

Femi: Ma, I'll like to help too

Mrs Ola: *[laughs]* don't worry dear, you don't need to

Femi: But I'd love to

Mrs Ola: I don't know if you can...

Femi*: [interrupts]* I Know you are doubtful of my ability to do the chores because you know I don't do them at home, but if you will permit me I can learn to do them here

Mrs Ola*: [Amazed]* Oh dear, ok then I will let you, but just do the little you can, all right?

Femi*: [smiles]* Alright ma, thanks for giving me a chance
[The three of them Kunle, Tinu and Femi all fetched water into all the jars and they were all happy together, as for Femi it was one of the happiest moment of his life he had always admire, but when they were done, Keji Femi's driver arrived, it was 4 p.m.]

Femi: Oh, My driver is here, I need to go now

Mrs Ola: You've tried today dear, please just wait and eat before leaving.

Femi: I'm sorry I won't be able to do that ma'am, I'm running late, I need to get home at least before 4:30 p.m. to avoid stories, bye ma

Mrs Ola: Oh, Ok dear, I wish you could stay but then...

Femi: Ok ma, I will come some other time to say Hello *[waves at Tinu and Kunle]* bye-bye

Tinu & Kunle: Bye Femi, love you!
[Femi hurries out into the car]

Curtain falls

ACT 6

SCENE 1

[After some weeks the first test commenced at Saint Jude high school, The test was done, script was marked, Mr Sam, the literature teacher came to distribute his script to the students]

Mr Sam: *[Faces the student]* I am not happy with your performance at all, imagine, only 10% of you did well in my test and remember literature is one of your core subject as an art student your performance isn't in any way encouraging!

Students: We are sorry sir

Mr Sam: No, you don't need to beg me, you should be begging yourselves to do better next time, anyway who is Femi Adejobi?

Femi: *[stands]* Yes sir

Mr Sam: Are you the new student that joined us this term?

Femi: Yes sir

Mr Sam: *[shakes his head]* Anyway class, he scored the highest mark in this test 16 marks of 20 A round of applause for him please [the class applauds] Keep it up boy you can have your seat anyway class, this is just your first test, you need to sit up and do better next time or else I won't take things easy with you, so let's call it a day!

[He leaves the class as the students appreciate, Immediately Mr Sam, left the class, Abbey walks up to Femi]

Abbey: Hi
Femi: Hello

Abbey: My name is Abiola Adams, but people call me Abbey

Femi: Nice to have you Abbey, I'm Femi Adejobi

Abbey: I know, Femi can you please explain to me, those tests questions, how to analyze those poems?

Femi: why not, it's my pleasure

Abbey: *[Brings out his note to jot as well as a literature test script and Femi explains to him, after the explanation Abbey was able to analyze the poems he couldn't analyze formerly and he did the corrections to his test]* Thank you Femi

Femi: You're welcome

Abbey: *[whispers to Femi]* Please just smile once in a while okay? [Before Femi could reply abbey was gone and Femi was left in amusement]*

ACT 6 SCENE 2

[Tinu sat all alone during the school break time and Femi

Femi: Hello Tinu

Tinu: Hello Femi, how're you?

Femi: I'm good and why are you here all alone? it's break time, you should be having fun with your friends.

Tinu: well, I just wish to be here

Femi: Ok, may I?

Tinu: please sit

Femi: Thanks, hmm.. There is this boy in our class called Abbey, he whispered to me just some moments ago to always smile once in a while what does he mean?

Tinu: it is just as it sounds

Femi: So I don't smile?

Tinu: well, it's rare to see you smile, since we've been together, I saw you smile only once.

Femi: *[Shocked]* You don't mean that!

Tinu: I honestly do

Femi: I'm sorry for that

Tinu: Not that Femi, just try to change, always smile, if not often at least when situations call for it please do. Femi:
Ok, I heard you. *[Leaves]*

Curtain falls

ACT 7

SCENE 1

[In the evening at Mr Adejobi's residence]

Mr Adejobi: *[Calls Femi]* Femi! Femi!

Femi: Yes Dad!

Mr Adejobi: Sit down, I want to have a discussion with you.

Femi: Now? Dad?

Mr Adejobi: Yes

Femi:*[Sits]* I'm all ears

Mr Adejobi*: [Clears his throat]* I'll be traveling to out of the country tomorrow to sort out some business issues.

Femi: *[suprised]* You'll be traveling tomorrow and you're just telling me this evening? Oh, Never mind, hope you've gotten your Visa ready?

Mr Adejobi: Yes!

Femi: How did you do that? I want to know, how did you communicate?

Mr Adejobi: That's none of your business, and besides your questions are getting unbearable, please take care of the house, that's all for now!

Femi:*[Goes into his room] [soliloquizing]* Why does this man hate me so much, he will be traveling tomorrow and he's just getting me informed this evening?, but how come I'm missing him all of a sudden, he didn't even tell me when he will return, how long   will   this   last!   Oh   God   help   me!

ACT 7 SCENE 2

[Kunle and Tinu decided to pay Femi a visit one saturday morning after learning that his father had gone on a business trip]

Kunle & Tinu: *[Press the bell at the gate, then kola rushes to see who it was]* Hello

Kola: Hi, Good afternoon, how may I help you?

Kunle: we're here to see Femi

Kola: *[surprised]* which Femi?

Tinu: Femi Adejobi

Kola: Are you sure?

Kunle: Yes sir, we are his friends, I am kunle and this is my sister Tinu

Kola: Oh, I see, but you can't see him now, come back some other time

Tinu: He told us he's home, we called his line before coming over!

Kola: He's busy, you can't see him now!

Kunle: You can put a call through to him, or better yet, go inside to confirm, he's expecting us

Kola: I said you can't see him, He doesn't need anyone's attention and besides he doesn't keep friends so how can you claim to be his friend?
[Femi saw the drama going on at the gate and didn't understand what was wrong so he decided to step out]

Femi: What's going on here, why...[sights Tinu and kunle] Oh, Tinu,
Kunle, you're here, I'm so happy to see you both, good evening, how're you?

Tinu& Kunle: we're fine

Tinu: We've been here for some couple of minutes now

Femi: Then why don't you come in?

Kunle*: [points at kola]* This man has been stopping us, claiming that you're busy and doesn't need anyone's attention.

Femi: *[Faces Kola]* When on earth did I tell you all this nonsense you just spitted out to my friends?

Kola: I'm sorry, I didn't know they were your friends

Tinu: *[Interrupt]* Liar we told you but you, were so bent on chasing us away

Kunle*: [Holds Tinu to calm her down]* it's okay

Femi: I'm sorry guys, I'm really sorry [Faces Kola] and you! Do you want to turn me into a masquerade that you'll hide and no one must see? Be careful!

Kola: I'm sorry sir

Femi: Not to me but to my friends!

Kola: *[To Kunle and Tinu]* I'm sorry

Kunle: it's okay

Femi: I'm so sorry guys, please, forgive me
Kunle: Oh no!, it's alright Femi

Femi: Ok then, let's go in please

Kunle: Wow! I must confess, your house is so big and beautiful!

Femi: Thank you, You both surprised me today, thanks alot
[They all moved to into the house]

Kunle: Wow! You're really a king here!

Femi: You think so?

Kunle: Yes, you have a gateman, cleaner, cook, maids..

Femi: *[interrupts]* but that's not the best of life, honestly it's really boring, you won't understand

Kunle: Then make me understand!

Femi: I really love your family, you are together doing things together and you are happy I think that's the best way to live.

Tinu: Hmm.. Don't you think you should also be grateful for what you have, you live in a big house you get all you want...

Femi: *[interrupts]*... Get all I wanted?...are you kidding? Of course you should be.

Tinu: I know, I understand but…

Femi: You don't understand, look at me here I was just a little boy of three(3) when my mum and dad got separated, no motherly affection, no one to correct when I do something wrong, I just live my life the way I know how, my father isn't even helping matters, he travels all the time and leaves me in care of maids' even when he's home, he nags and complain all the time, trying to forcefully bend me to his will, I struggle to educate myself, I am just grateful for the good people God surrounded me with otherwise I don't know what could have become of me, No parental care and affection and yet I live in a big mansion right? the son of the rich man! Isn't that what you mean?…

Kunle: *[Interrupts]* Femi please, stop! you need to stop being hard on yourself, you know you can always come to our house anytime you feel lonely instead of staying indoors here alone, you know you're always welcome

Femi: I know, and I'm grateful, I'm …**[Tisi, the cook, comes in to serve them food and drinks, which in turn interrupts their conversation]** Thank you

Tisi: Ok sir, is there anything else you need?

Femi: Yes, Get me a bottle of non-alcoholic wine

Tisi: Ok *[Tisi brings the wine and wanted to serve]*

Femi: Oh, no, don't worry, we'll serve ourselves, thanks, you may go now.

Tisi: Ok, enjoy yourselves

Kunle &Tinu: Alright, thank you ma'am
[They all ate and they was happy together]

Curtain falls

ACT 8

SCENE 1

[At St. Jude, Mr Jumo, the SS3 mathematics teacher enters the classroom]

Mr Jumo: Good morning class

Class: Good morning sir

Mr Jumo: well, this morning I'll give you some questions to solve; as you all know your external examination is fast approaching

Class: Yes sir

Mr Jumo: *[Wrote some questions on the board]* So, who will solve these? *[Some students came one after the other to solve the questions and they all solved them correctly]* Wow! this is good, I've always known you guys are brilliant! Applaud yourselves please! [Class applauds themselves]*

Mr Jumo: So now, I have a difficult question for you to solve, and there will be a reward for anyone who solves it correctly

Class: We will definitely solve it correctly!

Mr Jumo: Ok, we shall see

Femi: Yes Sir, I'll try [He examined the question for a while and made an attempt, then he stopped and faced the teacher] Sir, this question is unsolvable!

Mr Jumo: *[Surprised]* What do you mean?

Femi: The question is wrong, so it's unsolvable sir

Mr Jumo: *[Laughs]* So make it right then

Femi: *[Puts some signs that the teacher intentionally omitted, and solved the question, correctly;*
Mr Jumo: *[went silent for a while]* Has anyone ever told you that you're a genius? Applaud this boy please!

[The whole SS3 class applauds] [Mr Jumo ends the class took Femi to the principal's office and told the principal everything that happened and how he was able to solve a logical question and correct the errors. The principal Mr Oye, was surprised, checked his [Femi's] record right from his previous school, and discovered that he often make straight A's, such a brilliant student, an exam was set for him which he performed excellently well to the principal's dismay, he also had good recommendations from his teachers, all this made the school decided to give him a scholarship to continue his education abroad after completing the session, Femi was so happy at this offer, it was a life changing opportunity for him]

ACT 8 SCENE 2

[Femi became the talk of the school, as an announcement was made that afternoon to declare what has been decided by the school that very day; it was closing hour, and Kunle quickly rushes to Tinu and Femi's class]

Kunle: *[Hugs Femi]* Congratulations bro; I'd always knew you're great!

Femi: *[smiles]* Thank you, thanks alot

Tinu: Congratulations once again Femi

Femi: Thank you Kunle: it's 2:30pm already, Dad will be waiting,

[They all left the classroom to meet Mr Ola who was already waiting to take them home]

Tinu: *[Can't wait to break the news to her dad]* Dad, Femi got a scholarship Mr ola: Really?!

Kunle: Yes Dad, [kunle narrated everything to his father]

Mr Ola: *[Hugs Femi]* Oh, congratulations my boy

Femi: Thank you sir

Mr Ola: This calls for celebration

Kunle and Tinu: Yes Dad
[On their way home, they stopped by a restaurant to eat, and to   celebrate   Femi's   success]

ACT 8 SCENE 3

43

[Femi paid Mr Ola a visit; In Mr Ola's residence]
Mr Ola: Femi how are you? Congratulations once again, on your success

Femi: Thank you sir

Mr Ola: How's your dad?

Femi: He's fine sir

Mrs Ola: I'll come know your dad in person someday

Femi: Ok ma,..Oh, where's Kunle and Tinu I didn't sight them at all

Mrs Ola: I sent them to get me some stuffs, they will be back soon

Mr Ola: What brings you here Femi, to have fun with your friends?

Femi: Actually sir, I've been thinking about some things lately so I came to tell you about it

Mr Ola: Alright what's that?

Femi: It's about the scholarship I was given, I've been thinking about how to inform my dad, as this is almost the end of the second term of the session and if I would leave the country to study abroad, I was thinking he should know about it.

Mrs Ola: That's true

Mr Ola: Ok, so in respect that I will come and discuss that with your father during the holiday, You will start exam soon right?

Femi: Yes sir

Mrs Ola: when? **Femi:** In the next two weeks

Mr Ola: *[Turns to his wife]* Honey, so you see, you have to reduce or suspend some chores you give to this children *[Kunle*

and Tinu] so they can read for the coming exam since it's fast approaching.

Mrs Ola: Definitely! I'll do that

Mr Ola: Good, and Femi, prepare well for the exam

Femi: I will Sir

Mr Ola: *[recalls]* How is your dad, I thought you said he traveled sometimes ago is he back now?

Femi: Yes sir, he came back three days ago

Mr Ola: Okay, I'll come during the holiday to sort things out.

Femi: Thank you sir I'll really appreciate that; I'll love to take my leave now, please extend my greetings to Kunle and Tinu.
Mr & Mrs Ola: Alright

Curtain falls

ACT 9

SCENE 1

[During the holiday, Mr Ola visited the Adejobi's house, to discuss Femi's issue with his father as promised; after speaking with kola the gatekeeper, at the gate he was allowed into the compound]

Mr Adejobi: Good afternoon, how may I help you?

Mr Ola: Good afternoon sir, I'm Mr Ola Yemi, I came to inform you of your son's success.

Mr Adejobi: Oh really? Please sit, what success!?

Mr Ola: Thank you sir, As I was saying, your son has a remarkable reputation and excellent grade in school and as a result of this he has been…

Mr Adejobi: *[interrupts]* which of my son?

Mr Ola: Femi, sir

Mr Adejobi: Then I guess you don't know what you're talking about, did I hear you say school? If you're talking about school then you're not talking about my son, because my son has never been to school!

Mr Ola: And that is why I came sir, you have a very hard working and intelligent son, he's been schooling, he has cravings for education and so he finds his ways around it, he has been given…..

Mr Adejobi: *[Who has been sitting down watching patiently with amusement stood up all of a sudden, walks up to the door and opens it]* Mr Man, Get out!

Mr Ola: *[surprised]* Sir?!

Mr Adejobi: You heard me, I said get out!

Mr Ola: But I'm not through with the …..

Mr Adejobi: *[interrupts]* Out!

Mr Ola: *[Stood up and left the house in disappointment; Femi who has been eavesdropping the conversation comes out of his hiding place but before he could descend the stairs, Mr Ola has left]*

Femi: Dad!

Mr Adejobi: What?!

Femi: What is the meaning of this?

Mr Adejobi: Meaning of what?
[Femi left his father in the room and ran after Mr Ola, but he

is long gone so Femi took a taxi to his place to apologize for his father's rudeness]

ACT   9   SCENE   2

[After apologizing to Mr Ola, Femi went back to his father's house; He enters to go into his room]

Mr Adejobi: [Angry] …..And where do you think you are going?

Femi: To my room

Mr Adejobi: To your room? The house you built?

Femi: What?

Mr Adejobi: You heard me! Even your mum didn't contribute a penny to build this house, so what right did you have to enter this house?

Femi: *[surprised]* I am your son!

Mr Adejobi: Oh really?! So you still think you are my son after you disobeyed me, and did the unthinkable behind my back?

Femi: You should be glad I did this dad? You should be proud of me!

Mr Adejobi: Proud of you? For what? For the disregard you gave me? Or for making me look like a fool? Or for doing what I detest the most and didn't want you to do? You think you are smart right? but no, I am smarter. Now, go into that room, pack your clothes and get out of this house!

Femi: *[shocked!]* What!

Mr Adejobi: You heard me! Didn't you?

Femi: *[Almost weeping]* You can't do this!

48

Mr Adejobi: Well, I just did, I will not accommodate disrespect. No! Not from you! You are no longer my son, so get out of this house!

Femi: You can't mean this! Where do you expect me to go?

Mr Adejobi: To your father that sent you to school. If you don't get out of this vicinity in the next two hours, then I may be forced to do the unthinkable too!

Femi: Dad! *[Mr Adejobi ignores him so he went into the room to pick his box and left the house, Keji, Kola, Tisi and other nannies was very sorry about it but there was nothing they could do to help the situation]*

ACT 9 SCENE 3

[After Femi has left his father's house, he went to Mr Ola's house, no one was home except Tinu]

Femi: Good evening!

Tinu: *[surprised to see Femi with a big bag]* Hello Femi, what's going on, what's up with the bag?

Femi: My father disowned me

Tinu: *[shocked]* Why? Femi: I'm tired, May I please sit?

Tinu: Oh, sorry, my bad! Please sit, let me get you a cup of water. *[Tinu gave Femi a cup of cold water]*

Femi: Thanks.

Tinu: *[After a little silence, Tinu decided to speak]* Femi, explain to me, what happened? Why were you disowned by your father?

Femi: He got to know that I was schooling all the while, that's all.

Tinu: *[Recalls]* Oh! Dad explained everything before going back to the office, he'll be back soon; So you mean your dad disowned you for that reason?

Femi: *[Smiles Dryly]* Yes

Tinu: Oh no! So sorry Femi, Mum, Dad and Kunle will be back soon, but before then let me get you something to eat, just relax and feel free. *[Tinuke goes to the kitchen to make some food]*

Curtain falls

ACT 10

[Femi had gone to study abroad on scholarship, he was called to bar, he also came back to Nigeria to attend law school, did his LLB exam and was also called to bar in Nigeria, He's now a certified and famous lawyer who has won so many cases, he also won Young Professional award in Nigeria, due to his intelligence]

Femi: *[Knocks]* Hello

Mrs Ola: Yes, who's there?
[Opens the door]

Femi: Good afternoon ma

Mrs Ola: Good afternoon sir, how may I help you?

Femi: *[Moves closer]* it's me ma

Mrs Ola: *[Surprised]* Ah....Fe---emi!, How are you? Please, come in Femi: I'm fine ma,
[They embraced each other tightly, Mrs ola went in to call her husband, on seeing him, Femi prostrates] Good afternoon sir

Mr Ola: *[Excited]* Femi longest time, how're you? You're looking good

Femi: I'm good sir, thanks

Mr Ola: Ah, but Femi, why haven't you checked on us all the while since you've been back to Nigeria for almost 2 years now, that's not right, all we were hearing was your voice and your name over the media.

Femi: I'm really sorry, please forgive me, I just don't have an excuse, I'm sincerely sorry.

Mr Ola: Oh, no problem, we understand, You came back for your one year call to bar program and exams in Abuja, even coming from Abuja to this place isn't a small journey, we're glad to have you here dear, I'm so proud of you! Barrister Femi Adejobi..

Femi: Thanks for accepting my apology,

Mr Ola: *[Smiles]* By the way, let me put a call through to Tinu and Kunle to come over.

Femi: I've actually done that sir, we've discussed on phone they said they'll soon be here.

Mr Ola: Case settled, we didn't know that you've contacted yourselves

Femi: We've sure done that, *[After a while, Kunle enters, greeted his parents while he and Femi hugged each other tightly]*

Kunle: I'm sorry, I'm a little bit late Barrister, I had to attend to some patient urgently.

Femi: Never mind Doctor, I understand.

Kunle: Hmm..Let me explain myself before I get sued to court! *[They all laughed at Kunle's joke]*

Femi: So, how about Tinu? I called her too,

Kunle: She'll be here shortly.

Femi: I've missed you all, I'm so glad to see you again!

Kunle: We're glad to see you too.
[Tinu enters in a short while, greets her parents and brother, she hugs Femi]

Tinu: Barrister Femi, How're you?

Femi: I'm fine Journalist, how have you been?

Tinu: I've been fine, can't you see I'm looking fresh?

Femi: *[Laughs]* I can see that! Good to see you..

Tinu: And I, you

Mrs Ola: So my children, I've made some special delicacies for your coming, the dining is set, so let's all go to the dining table to eat our lunch, after then, we can continue this discussion.

Kunle: I agree with you mum!
[They all ate lunch; and after that, Mr Ola starts the conversation]

Mr Ola: Ehn..en Femi, have you heard from your father?

Femi: *[Surprised]* Father? Which father?

Mr Ola: Mr Adejobi of course!

Femi: Oh... I'm sorry, what about him?

Mr Ola: So you mean, you've not been hearing from him all the while?

Femi: Yes ma'am, I've lost his contacts, he's still alive right?

Mr Ola: Of course! What kind of statement is that?

Femi: Ugh..I'm sorry sir, but I just asked a question

Mrs Ola: We know you're still angry with him Femi, how come our happy Femi switched mood and suddenly became angry after the mention of his father's name! *[Laughs]*

Mr Ola: But to be honest with you Femi, he really needs help!
Femi: He should go ahead and get helped, I'm not stopping him.

Mr Ola: *[smiles]* I think it's high time you forgive your father

Femi: Oh...

Mrs Ola: To tell you the truth, he's going through a though time right now, and let me also not forget to tell you that, he has apologized for what he did the other day

Femi: Really? How come?

Mr Ola: Yes, he came to apologize after some month, then he asked if we knew where you might be, but unfortunately for him, you were no longer in the country at that time.

Mrs Ola: I think he's realized everything he did, you really need to forgive him.

Femi: But it's too late ma'am, why should I forgive someone who disowned me? why should I forgive someone who didn't care for me, and caused me hardship as a teenager, I don't think I can do that, I'm sorry!

Mr Ola: *[Moves closer to Femi and put a hand round his neck]*You really need to forgive your father

Kunle: Yes Femi, Apart from realizing his mistakes, he was also hospitalized some months ago, he has a high BP, he was admitted for some weeks before he was discharged, and in some of my calls, I attended to him, his health is failing!

Femi: *[shocked]* Really! but how's he now?

Kunle: Well, he got better a little bit before we had him discharged, and he was placed on medications

Femi: Ok then,

Tinu: Not only that Femi, his story is all over the internet presently, and right now as I'm speaking, your Dad is in prison.

Femi: *[shocked]* Impossible! That can't be true! How come? Why will he be in prison?!, he may be hot-headed I know, but he's not a criminal, how come? Why?

Tinu: We actually don't know yet! we're still on it and as a journalist I had a chance to speak with him once or twice on this, and from his words, it's like he's been framed for a crime he didn't commit as regarding his company, and with the way things are right now, your dad can't even get a lawyer, he's as poor as a church rat, all he had has been taken away from him..

Femi: Impossible!

Mr Ola: So you see why you need to forgive your father and help him as well.

Femi: Oh God! what's this?

Mr Ola: So you'll need to visit him in prison to find out all about this issue!
[Draws   him   closer   and   hugs   him]

ACT   10   SCENE   2

[The next day Mr Ola, His Wife and Femi went to see Mr Adejobi in prison]

Mr Adejobi: Mr Ola, I'm really glad to see you thanks for checking up on me

Femi: Good afternoon Sir,

Mr Adejobi: Good afternoon young man, please sit,

Mr Ola: I'm sorry I've not been coming for some time is now, I've been busy lately

Mr Adejobi: No problem, Thanks for always coming and thanks for not abandoning me, Oh, Who is this young man?

Mr Ola: *[Surprised]* You mean this? *[Pointing to Femi]*

Mr Adejobi: Yes,

Mr Ola: *[Amused]* But this is...

Femi: *[Interrupts]* I'm a lawyer

Mr Adejobi: *[Excited]* Oh, Mr Ola, you finally got me a lawyer, thank you so much

Mr Ola: *[Short of words, as he didn't understand what was going on with Femi, and why he introduced himself in that manner]* You're welcome

Femi: So what happened, the rumor going on is that you embezzled money in your company and also borrowed some huge loans which you failed to return

Mr Adejobi: Honestly young lawyer, I didn't borrow or embezzle any money from the company..

Femi: So, what brought you here then, I need you to tell me the whole truth.

Mr Adejobi: Actually Sir, I had some argument with one of my most trusted workers, he has been working with me for a long time and I trusted him so much, I usually entrust the company to his care whenever I'm not in the country, he is more educated and experienced than I am, and he is smart, So, whenever I travel out of the country, I put him in charge, After the argument, He apologized and I forgave him, some weeks later, I received an urgent call from Dubai that my attention was needed regarding the company, so I entrusted the company into his care like I always did, but this time I didn't know he had other intentions, and to my uttermost dismay, before I came back from that trip, He had borrowed a huge sum of money in the company's name and ran out of the country, so I was arrested and all that I had including my house, the filling stations and industries were seized

Femi: This is ridiculous! How could you do such a thing? Don't you know how risky it is to entrust your life to another man? A company for that matter?

Mr Adejobi: He has been the one helping me with the management of the company all the while, he is educated and more experienced than I am, I stopped schooling at basic six(6) he knew this, and this was why he could you use it to play on me.

Femi: Hmm..So how exactly did you know that he did all this?

Mr Adejobi: He put a call through to me recently, and mockingly told me all he did.

Femi: On which phone please?

Mr Adejobi: I can't actually recollect but I know that a phone was given to me to speak to someone which turned out to be him.

Femi: By who? Please you need to think about this, who exactly gave you the phone? You just need to think!

Mr Adejobi: *[Burst into tears]* I really don't remember sir,

Femi: it's Ok, Calm down, this matter will be re-investigated, thanks for your cooperation.
[Femi taps Mr and Mrs Ola who has been sitting there listening to the conversation in amusement and they all left]

ACT   *10*   *SCENE*   *3*

[Barrister Femi met with one of the prison warder and spoke with him to please help in search of the cell phone which was used to put a call through to Mr Adejobi while in prison, the phone was gotten and it was taken to the mobile phone operators and the conversation was tracked and recorded the conversation between Mr Adejobi and Mr Ben was tracked and Mr Ben was traced and arrested then Mr Adejobi's case was revisited, with Femi standing as the lawyer; Mr and Mrs Ola as well as Mr Jerry, was also at the court; After visiting the case, Mr Adejobi was discharged and acquainted, he was so happy]

Mr Adejobi: *[Faces Mr Ola]* Thank you Mr Ola, thanks for all you did for me, *[Faces Femi]* Young lawyer thank you thanks for defending me thank you so much.

Femi: You're welcome sir

Mr Adejobi: Mr Ola, thanks for being there with me when no one was, thanks for getting me a lawyer thank you very much

Mr Ola: Don't mention it, you're welcome but Mr Kole, did you recognize this person? *[points to Femi]*

Mr Adejobi: Oh yes I do, lawyer, thank you so much for helping me, may the good Lord bless you

Femi: Amen

Mr Ola: Oh, Mr Kole Adejobi, that still doesn't answer my question.

Mr Adejobi: Of course I do recognize him, He is the young lawyer that helped me with the investigation and revisiting of my case and also, he defended me in court today, I recognize him, I do! I owe you my life lawyer thank you very much *[wants to prostrate]*

Femi:*[Holds his father to stop him from prostrating]* Stop it father!

Mr Adejobi: Lawyer, Did I just hear you say Father? How sweet it is for a lawyer like you to call me father, I'm so happy thank you...Oh lawyer you just reminded me of my son, How I destroyed myself with some stupid fables in my head, how I denied my son the opportunity that everyone has, not because I wasn't wealthy enough back then, and yet I disowned him! Oh, I was such a bad father to him, I don't know what he could have become if I had permitted him to be educated
[Bursts into tears]

Mr Jerry: Yes Kole but today isn't the day you should weep, I could remember you always told me that your son will inherit your wealth when you are old and gone, but now, where is the wealth?

You couldn't even manage the wealth well for him to inherit, yet you refused him formal education; oh what a life!

Mr Adejobi: *[Weeping profusely]* Ah! Jerry; I'm sorry, I should have listened to you but my pride won't let me

Mr Jerry: Ah! Femi! how I've missed that boy so much, A child with a promising future so wise and intelligent, talented beyond his years. I just hope he's safe wherever he is, and as for you Kole, I don't think I can forgive you for letting the boy off like that!

Mr Ola: *[Who has been watching in amusement spoke up]* Sir, I don't think you also recognize this lawyer?

Mr Jerry: Oh, I do, lawyer thank you so much for your help, In fact you are an angel sent to us, I don't know what we could have done without you, thank you very much, You see lawyer what we are saying here is that my friend also has a son, I think he should be about your age now, but my friend here disowned him.

Femi: So where's the boy now?

Mr Jerry: I never heard of him since he left home, I just miss him and hope he is safe wherever he is.

Mrs Ola: *[Smiles]* So, you won't recognize him when you see him too?

Mr Jerry: The last time I saw him was when he was 17, I don't know if I could still....

Mr Ola: *[Interrupts]* But this is the boy!

Mr Jerry: what did you mean?

Mr Ola: This is Femi; The lawyer is your son Mr Adejobi.

Mr Adejobi: What did you just say?

Mr Ola: Yes, you heard me right, This is Femi, the barrister that helped you today was the son you disowned!

Mr Jerry: *[Stares at Femi for a while, then walks up to him and hug him]* Femi! is this really you?

Femi: Yes sir,

Mr Jerry: *[Hugs him again]* You finally made it! I'm so proud of you!

Femi: *[Smiles]* Thank you sir, thank for all the help you rendered back then, what could I have done without you.

Mr Jerry: Oh! don't mention, you deserved it! *[calls his friend]* Kole come and hug your son

Mr Adejobi: *[Breaks into tears once again as he reluctantly moves towards Femi]* I'm so sorry, I know I don't deserve your forgiveness, but I'm sorry, pl..ea..se

Femi: *[Looks at his father and Hugs him]* it's Okay, d--a--d

Mr Adejobi: Thank you, thanks for calling me Dad, My Son, I'm sorry for the hardship I made you go through, for my foolishness, I am so sorry.
Femi: *[wipes his father's tears with his handkerchief and hugs him]* It's ok Dad, I have forgiven you I have truly forgiving you.

Mrs Ola: I'm so proud of you dear

Mr Adejobi: Thank you, thanks for your forgiveness even when I don't deserve it, Oh! I'm so sorry, I've done so much wrong

Mr Ola: The boy has forgiven you Mr Kole, but you need to forgive yourself and let the past go, Yes, you did him wrong, but that made him stronger, see the positive side of things and let the past go, and Femi thanks for not giving up even when you had all the reason to, I'm so proud of you, thanks for sticking to your dreams despite all odds!

Femi: [*Faces Mr and Mrs Ola]* Thank you also Sir and Ma for being an angel of God sent to me, for your help, parental advice and prayers that kept me going.

Mr & Mrs Ola: Don't mention it dear, we are so proud of you; Thank God

Femi: *[Faces Mr Jerry]* Thank you also sir, for your guidance and help, for not giving up on me, you're such an Angel!

Mr Jerry: Don't mention it dear, thanks for proving me right.

Femi: [Looks at his father and hug him] It's okay Dad, things will get back to place, as for your company and some other things will be returned back to you, Mr Benson your friend, was traced and has been arrested, he has confessed all he did to the police as that phone call was also an evidence against him, so with time some of the things you've lost will be returned to you, if not fully but some. Things will be fine.
[They hugged each other]

THE END

ABOUT THE AUTHOR

TAIWO EUNICE BEJIDE

Taiwo .E. Bejide, is a passionate young Lady, born in the capital city of ondo state Nigeria, Akure precisely into the family of Mr.&Mrs Bejide Victor. She had her primary school education at Shalom Integrated Nur|Pry. school and her secondary Education at St. Louis Girls Grammar School Akure as an Arts student where she discovered her love for writing; she then proceeded to Adekunle Ajasin University, where she studied Linguistics and Languages and graduated with Bachelor of Art Honours; She also possess diploma in Human Resource Management, Journalism and Mass Media, among others.